Chapter

1
The bed

It was a very strange bed. Jenny's father had found it at the back of an old junk shop. It was almost hidden by ancient tennis rackets and dusty pictures. When the shop-owner cleared them away, Mr Lockhart could see at once that it was just what they had been searching for. Ever since Jenny's old one had broken he had been looking for a cheap, narrow bed to fit her thin, long room. There were not many ways of arranging the furniture without bumping into it. Jenny always had bruises on her legs.

Mr Lockhart thought the new bed was just the right size, even if it did look a bit odd. Jenny's parents struggled up the stairs with it while she followed.

"It's a bit weird," she said.

"I know," agreed Dad. "But as soon as I saw it I knew it was the kind of bed you'd like. I thought – Jenny's weird too. She's bound to like this one."

"Thanks very much, Dad!" Jenny grinned and

pushed a few curls of vivid red hair from her eyes.

Her parents staggered round the top of the stairs and finally managed to squeeze through the doorway into Jenny's bedroom. She had already cleared a space and it did not take long to push the bed snugly against one wall. Everyone stepped back and gazed at it.

"Isn't it tall?" Mum said. "I've never seen a bed like it in my life." Her husband leaned forward and ran one hand along the wooden frame.

"I think it's pretty old. The shopkeeper said he thought it may have come from a ship. I suppose the high sides stopped sailors falling out of bed in a storm."

Jenny held the sides of her new bed and smiled. It was the best bed she had ever seen. Her father was still pointing things out.

"The man in the shop said he'd been told there was some kind of secret cupboard but he had never found it. I think there are some carvings underneath."

In a flash Jenny was crawling under the bed. Her eyes had just got used to the dark when a strange feeling swept over her. It was almost as if she was in two places at once. It felt weird. If she looked out she could see her mother's feet in her silly slippers with the blue pom-poms. Her parents' voices sounded like a TV programme heard through next-door's wall.

Jenny turned her head to look at the scratchings in the wood. There were mostly initials. On one plank there were several drawings of old ships with full sails, carved into the wood. Jenny traced them with a finger. She could almost hear the crash of water against the bows. A shiver ran up her spine. She poked her head out into the daylight.

"What do you think?" asked Mum. "We know you wanted a new bed, but money's a bit short and..."

"I know it's a bit odd," apologized Dad. Jenny beamed up at her parents.

"It's wonderful. The old wood is really nice. I bet hundreds of sailors have slept in it."

"Not all at the same time, I dare say," laughed Mum. "Anyhow, I'm glad you like it. I have to admit it *is* unusual. You can put the sheets on, can't you? We'll leave you to it."

Jenny waited until they had left the room. She quietly shut her bedroom door and looked back at her strange bed. The sheets would have to wait. There were more important things to be done. She wriggled back beneath the bed. How could she find that secret cupboard? Jenny lay on her back in the darkness, staring into the gloom.

At first all seemed silent and still, but after a minute or two she began to hear the faintest sounds. A creaking murmur came and went, rising and falling. Jenny thought for a second that the floor moved beneath her, but surely that was impossible! Most of all there was a strong feeling that the bed was trying to tell her something. At odd moments she was sure she heard voices. In that eerie darkness she sensed danger and excitement.

A gust of salty wind suddenly blew across her face and she panicked. She scrambled out into her bedroom.

Her heart was pounding. She put a hand to her cheek where the wind had touched it. She looked at her bedroom window but it was firmly shut.

Jenny stared at the bed. There was certainly something very odd about it. If it felt strange when she was under the bed, what would it be like to sleep in?

2
Night time

It was ages before Jenny fell asleep. Maybe it was because she was expecting something, hoping for something. She turned over and over, trying to get comfortable. Her pillows felt like wooden boxes. Her duvet coiled itself round her feet like a soft octopus.

At last sleep did come. It came like white clouds that build slowly in the sky, growing larger and larger, taking out more and more of the daylight. With the clouds came white spots that seemed to swoop across the insides of her eyelids. They were there when her eyes were shut. If she sleepily opened her eyes they vanished at once. Closing her eyes brought them back, swooping and rising, thin triangles of white – like gulls.

There was a tang in the air. The old bed rocked Jenny to sleep, lulling her with the sound of waves lapping at a ship. The wind filled the great, grey sails. Spray flew from the plunging bow and whipped across the deck, scattering the sunlight like flung diamonds.

The gulls followed for a long time, keeping up with the ship, hardly moving their wings. Jenny watched them rise and fall in the sky until they gradually fell back, turning for home. The ship was out of sight of land.

Jenny shut her cabin door and went up the wooden steps to the main deck. Sweaty men were running backwards and forwards. Everyone seemed busy. Some were hauling on ropes. Some were climbing the rigging. Jenny watched with astonishment, but before she even had time to think,

a gruff shout in her ear made her jump.

"Oi! You! Get to work, you lazy little stinker, before I fry your liver!"

Jenny found herself staring into a huge, bearded, blotchy face. "Come on! Shake a leg and get up that rigging!" Jenny didn't need telling twice. She scrambled up the thick rope ladder to help with the sails. She was trying so hard to make it look as if she knew what she was doing that she did not even have time to think about where she was. When at last the heavy canvas puffed out with wind, Jenny gazed round.

Nothing but sea! The boat heaved and rolled. The sailors got on with their tasks. Up on the quarter-deck stood a giant of a man, naked to the waist. He was gripping the handles of the big wheel, with fists the size of melons.

Next to him was a slim, wiry woman. She was leaning over the rail and watching the crew at work. She had a constant, slightly cruel smile. Her hair was a flaming red mass of curls. The sea wind caught and tossed the long strands so that they seemed to writhe about her head as if they were alive.

At that moment the woman looked up and saw Jenny. Her smile froze. She straightened up quickly.

The alarm clattered beside her bed. Jenny sat up, rock-like, breathing fast. She looked around, expecting to see the ship's crew at work. No... there was nothing but her bedroom. She turned off the alarm and felt the smooth, dark wood of her bed. Slowly she got up and put on her slippers.

"Wow!" she murmured to herself.

"Sleep well?" asked Mrs Lockhart, when Jenny went downstairs.

"Brilliant! I've been at sea all night!"

Her mother smiled and set the table for breakfast.

Jenny sat there dreamily, her head filled with memories of her night at sea. Was it a dream, or had it really happened?

"Jenny!" Mum cried. "You're slopping your cereal down your chin! Your thoughts must have been miles away! Wipe your face quickly now, it's almost time for school. Don't forget your packed lunch."

Jenny's thoughts were brought back to earth with a bang. School – she had to go to school. She picked up her lunch-box and set off up the road. Half-way there her feet began to drag. She was scared. What would happen today? What new misery would spoil everything yet again?

"Hey, it's Ketchup-Head!" shouted Vicky, running across the playground with her two friends close behind. Vicky patted Jenny's flame-red hair. "Ketchup-Head," she repeated. "You don't mind being called that, do you? Of course not. It's an excellent name." Jenny tried to back away but Sharon grabbed her elbow.

"No, don't go away. We're your friends."

"Yeah, friends," muttered Clare. Sharon grinned at the others.

"What have you got for lunch? Something tasty?"

Jenny held tightly onto her lunch-box. "I don't know. I haven't looked."

"Oh!" squealed Vicky. "Ketchup-Head hasn't looked! Never mind. We're your friends, so we'll look for you!" Sharon tore the lunch-box from Jenny's fingers.

"Hey! Give that back! It's my lunch!" started Jenny.

"Keep your hair on," Vicky said, with a smirk. "We'll look after it for you, won't we? Oh, look, a chocolate bar. You don't want that getting into the wrong hands, do you?" Vicky slipped it into her own pocket.

"Crisps!" cried Sharon. "Isn't it nice to share things with your friends?" She took out the apple that Jenny's mum had packed and handed it to Clare. Sharon snapped the box shut and tossed it back to Jenny, whose face was absolutely white.

Jenny clenched her hands into tight fists, but she couldn't use them. Her eyes were full of tears that she fought to keep back. Sharon pressed Jenny back against the wall and smiled very sweetly at her.

"Don't forget, we're your friends," she hissed.

"We look after you," added Vicky. "Without us, something nasty might happen, especially if you tell anyone." The gang started to move away.

"Oh – thanks for the lunch!" shouted Sharon, and they ran off, giggling, to the other end of the playground. Jenny shut her eyes as tightly as she could. A single tear appeared on her left cheek. She quickly brushed it away.

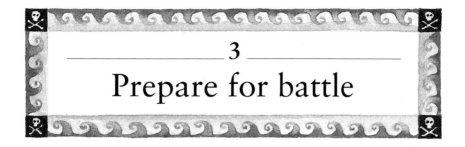

3
Prepare for battle

"How was school?" asked Mum when Jenny got home. Jenny carried her lunch-box through to the kitchen and slid it quietly onto the side.

"Okay."

"That's what you say every day. I never know what's happening these days. Is everything all right?"

"It's okay," insisted Jenny. She quickly went and sat in front of the television and turned the sound up. Her mother sighed and gave up asking, much to Jenny's relief.

She stared at the screen, but her thoughts were miles away at sea. The actors on television might just as well have been speaking Russian. Jenny wasn't listening or looking. She was thinking about the look on that woman's face as their eyes met. There had been a flash of something, almost as if they recognized each other. How could that be? Everything had happened in such a rush. One moment she had been at sea and then her alarm clock went off. Whole hours seemed like minutes, or was it the other way round?

Then there was Jenny's other problem – school. Her mind filled with a deep, grey despair. She didn't know how to handle it. At one time Clare had been Jenny's best friend, but the other two, Sharon and Vicky, had stolen her away. Sharon and Vicky had a habit of stirring things at school. The other children did not like them for it.

Over the last couple of weeks all three of them had taken to calling Jenny "Ketchup-Head" because of her thick, flame-red curls. There were times when Jenny hated her hair.

The trio made a point of pestering her. They bumped into her. They hid her books and broke her pencils. Jenny didn't know why they did these things and she never told anyone. This just made the problem worse, but Jenny didn't want to get Clare into trouble. It hurt to see her old friend mixed up with Vicky and Sharon.

Mrs Lockhart called her for tea. She was very hungry, having had most of her lunch stolen, and she did feel much better after eating. She went to bed hoping that tomorrow would be a better day. Maybe Clare would feel guilty and want to be her friend again. Maybe nothing would happen. Meanwhile, she had her new bed to look forward to. Where would Jenny be tonight?

The moment she entered her bedroom she was in a different world. She stood by the door for several seconds, trying to place where she was. She could feel the door frame with one hand. She could see her clothes scattered across the floor. But her room was filled with a stiff sea breeze. Distant, urgent noises filled her ears and at the back of her bedroom she was sure she could see the heaving ocean.

Jenny hurried to her bed as the floor pitched and rolled beneath her unsteady feet. She sat upright, clutching the covers. Large waves hammered on the side of the creaking ship. The wind drove against the great hull, making it tilt to one side. Jenny was startled by a thunderous knocking on her cabin door. It burst open. A grim, bearded sailor waved a pistol at her.

"Come on, young monkey!" he bellowed. "It's no good hiding in bed. Captain Skull will skin you alive! Up on deck and quick about it, before Snakehair sees you and has you whipped!"

The sailor vanished up the steps, leaving Jenny wondering who these people were. Captain Skull? Snakehair? Why were they after her? Jenny slipped from the bed and followed the sailor up to the main deck. What chaos! The crew charged about, rolling back cannons and loading them. Gun ports were thrown open. Piles of weapons appeared on the deck. The crew stared across the port side. A second ship was bearing down on them under full sail.

A sharp cry came from the quarter-deck. Jenny looked round and there was the woman with flaming hair, slashing the air with a sword and roaring commands at her crew.

"Raise the flag! Tarbuck, fetch my pistol! More sail aloft!" She ran to the port side and cursed violently. Then she saw Jenny. Her eyes flashed as she tossed back her writhing red curls. A smile, half cruel, came and went.

"Don't stand there like a cow waiting to be milked, Jenny! Here – catch!" Snakehair snatched up a sword and threw it down. Much to Jenny's surprise she caught it without even thinking. It was as easy as picking up a table-knife.

The enemy ship was much closer. Jenny could see the men on board arming themselves for battle. Her heart jumped as she spotted a skull-and-crossbones fluttering from the main mast. Pirates! Automatically she glanced up at her own ship's flag and this time her heart almost fell out of her mouth. Another skull-and-crossbones! So they were pirates too!

Jenny gripped her sword. The entire ship shook from stem to stern as the cannons thundered. Black and grey smoke drifted across the deck.

"Stand by to board ship!" yelled Snakehair, above the mounting din. She was half-way up the rigging, spyglass to one eye. "It's Captain Skull all right, lads – him and his scurvy mob of yellow-bellies! They'll be after our treasure! Give them no quarter! It's to the death, men – to the death!" Snakehair grinned wildly and leaped lightly down to the deck.

The two ships were almost touching and Jenny could see the tense, fierce faces of the enemy. The ships seemed to lurch away from each other for a few seconds, then there was a great grinding and splintering as they crashed together. A mighty roar of voices exploded from both ships as the pirates flung themselves upon each other.

A shrill ringing burst into Jenny's ears. She sat upright, panting and sweating. She stared blankly around her bedroom while the ringing went on and on. Jenny blinked and rubbed her eyes. Her heart was still pounding. She reached out and switched off the alarm. Silence filled the room. It was half past seven. Time to get up. She must have been at sea all night.

4
Close encounters

"Oh, look," cried Vicky, barring Jenny's path. "Lunch has arrived!"

Jenny paled and her heart began to race. She glanced behind to see if she could escape that way, but Sharon quickly slipped behind her.

"Too slow!" laughed Sharon, then leaned forward and whispered menacingly into Jenny's ear. "There's no escape."

Vicky took charge. "So, what have you got today, then? It had better be something good. Hand it over." Jenny clutched her lunch-box close to her chest. Her face was tight and drawn. Vicky stepped forward.

"I said hand it over, Ketchup-Head."

Sharon suddenly grabbed Jenny's arms and pinned them to her sides. Jenny looked hopefully at Clare but her ex-friend just stood biting her lower lip. Vicky grinned and took the lunch-box from Jenny's hands.

"Thank you so much," she mocked. "You're so

kind. Oh look, cheese sandwiches. And crisps – oh
dear – beef flavour." Vicky glared at Jenny. "I
thought we told you to get cheese and onion? It had
better be cheese and onion next time or it will be the
gangplank for you. Still, this will do. Ta very much."
The girls walked off.

"Hey!" cried Jenny. "You've still got my lunch-
box."

"Yeah, nice, isn't it?" laughed Sharon, and the
three girls disappeared round the corner.

By the end of the afternoon the box was still missing. Jenny did not dare ask again. She went home without it and of course it was the first thing that her mother noticed.

"I left it at school," mumbled Jenny. Mum sighed.

"You'll have to have a polybag tomorrow. You haven't lost it, have you?"

"No!"

Mrs Lockhart glanced at her daughter in surprise, then shrugged and went back to the garden to finish the pruning.

All evening Jenny was jumpy. Her father and mother both noticed. They kept glancing at each other and trying to prompt Jenny into talking, but Jenny was silent. What on earth was she supposed to say? How about: "Well, you see, Dad, the problem is, I've got all these pirates in my bedroom fighting each other." Dad would just laugh then, and Jenny didn't think she could bear that.

At last she went upstairs. She paused outside her bedroom door. She counted to ten, took a deep breath and opened the door. Choking smoke filled her lungs and the strong, exciting smell of exploded gunpowder made her heart beat faster. A brawny sailor banged against her as he ran past. The smoke drifted slowly on the wind. Jenny glanced up at the quarter-deck.

A tremendous battle was taking place. Flashing swords clashed in the air. Snakehair was fighting for her life, cornered by three roaring pirates. One of them was obviously Captain Skull, for he was tall and gaunt and the skin on his face was drawn tightly

over his bones. A long scar ran down one cheek. Snakehair cried out as a thin blade opened a wound on her leg.

Jenny didn't waste any time. Snatching up a sword she rushed up the steps and dashed forward, throwing herself upon the gang. Snakehair was too busy to cast Jenny more than a glance, but her eyes sparked as she saw Jenny fly to her rescue.

One of the pirates gave a curse and turned. His sword blade swung across Jenny's face. She took a quick step back then darted forward, her own blade cutting the air and driving the sweating giant back. Now he was struggling to stop Jenny's advance. Back he went, cursing at every step, until he was stopped by the railings. He could go back no further. Jenny drove forward with her sword. The pirate gave a terrified yell, plunged over the railings and hit the sea with a resounding smack.

Snakehair was in deep trouble. Even though Jenny had rid her of one attacker, the other two were crowding in on her. Snakehair was a superb swordswoman but she was slowly being driven into a corner from where there was no escape. She managed to spear one pirate's arm, but at that same moment Captain Skull leaped forward and grabbed her, seizing her sword and flinging it away.

Jenny was just in time to see the enemy captain dragging Snakehair away. All around her a frenzy of fighting went on. Jenny pushed her way through the struggling bodies, trying to reach Snakehair, but Captain Skull had already forced her down below.

Nobody else seemed to have noticed. Jenny realized that she was the only person who could save Snakehair now. She gripped her sword and slipped quietly down the steps and into the gloomy passageway to the cabins.

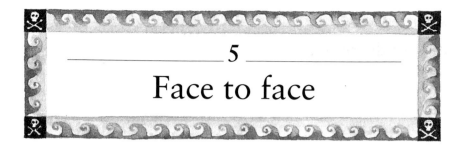

5
Face to face

Jenny stopped at the bottom of the steps. She held her breath and listened. She was not certain which cabin they were in. She hid in the shadows. From the other side of one door came the sound of loud voices.

"So where is the treasure, my lovely?" demanded Captain Skull, the tip of his sword a few centimetres from Snakehair's throat. She tossed back her red curls and almost spat at him.

"Do you think I'd tell a sea-slug like you?"

Captain Skull gave a snort of laughter and waved his sword in front of her face.

"It won't take me long to find out."

Jenny gripped the door latch and lifted it very carefully. She pushed the door open a crack. Captain Skull had his thin back to her. Jenny opened the door a little wider and squeezed silently into the cabin. Snakehair saw Jenny creep in but forced herself not to look. She held Captain Skull's eyes with her own,

sneering at her enemy, while Jenny crept round the
edge of the room.

"Where's the map?" thundered Captain Skull. Snakehair grinned back at him.

"You'll never know, you fat octopus!"

"By the devil I'll find out! I'll make you tell me if it's the last thing I do!" Captain Skull drew back his sword and at that moment Jenny stepped forward.

"It *will* be the last thing you do, Captain Skull," she said, with dangerous calm. The pirate chief whirled round and his look of utter astonishment thrilled Jenny.

"Another one!" he growled. "And a child at that. I'm going to skewer you both on my sword like kebabs!"

His sword darted forward and the blade clashed with Jenny's. She jumped to one side but he pounced after her. The swords whirled and danced in the air. Chairs went flying as Captain Skull plunged across the room. Sparks flew from the crashing blades. Then just as Captain Skull thought Jenny was helpless she sprang forward, taking him completely by surprise.

Her thin sword blade became a blur, dazzling the captain and forcing him back. Jenny lunged forward. Her blade passed clean through the pirate's sleeve and pinned him against the wall. His sword fell with a clatter. Snakehair snatched it up with a cry of triumph and waved it under Captain Skull's thin nose.

"Fine work, Jenny! Look what we've caught! A gibbering jellyfish with no sting left! My thanks to you, young Jenny! Now, slug, get up those stairs or you'll be walking the gangplank before you know it!"

They pushed Captain Skull ahead of them and up onto the quarter-deck. As soon as the others saw that their chief had been captured they threw down their weapons and gave themselves up. The battle was over and won. Snakehair's crew took the prisoners down to the hold, while Snakehair ran a quick eye over her boat and made sure that the wounded were seen to.

A small crew went aboard Captain Skull's ship and it followed closely. Snakehair pushed a wave of red curls away from her eyes and glanced at Jenny.

"I won't forget what you did," she said. "I'll make it up to you. One day I shall be there to help you." Jenny was silent, her eyes held by Snakehair's burning gaze. "There's a tiger in your heart Jenny – a tiger like the one in mine. Never forget that. You take care now…"

But Jenny heard no more. Her ears were full of ringing and she opened her eyes. She was in bed, in her own room. The alarm was going again.

"Phew!" she murmured to herself, and switched it off. It was early morning.

During breakfast Mrs Lockhart put a polybag packed with food on the table.

"This will have to do today, Jenny. Do bring your lunch-box back. It was expensive and really we can't manage without it." Jenny was brought back sharply to the real world. She'd practically forgotten about the three playground pirates. She muttered "Yeah…" to her mother and set off for school.

Vicky, Clare and Sharon were waiting on the path to the playground. Vicky grinned and nudged the others as Jenny appeared.

"Oh dear, no lunch-box. What can have happened to your lovely lunch-box? Surely you haven't lost it?"

"Shame! Poor little Ketchup-Head has lost her lunch-box and doesn't know where to find it," sang Sharon. "But what a dinky little polybag you've got. Let's see what you've brought us, then. It had better not be beef crisps again," she threatened. The three girls closed in round Jenny.

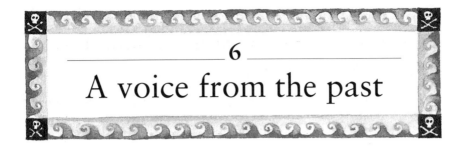

6
A voice from the past

Jenny's heart pounded against her ribs. Not again!
Her eyes went from one girl to another. They
smirked back at her. Then all at once a voice came
into Jenny's head and she thought she could see
another face… slim, wind-tanned and covered with
flaming curls.

"There's a tiger in your heart, Jenny," said the
voice. "A tiger just like mine."

Jenny looked back at the three girls, but this time
the gang shifted their feet uneasily. Jenny pushed
some stray red hair from her face. The curls were like
coiling snakes beneath her fingers. She felt a fierce
smile growling deep inside. She stepped forward,
closer to Vicky.

"Just where is my lunch-box?" she demanded
coldly.

Vicky's astonishment was as thrilling to watch as
Captain Skull's. This was something she had never

expected. Vicky attempted a smile.

"Oh dear, does poor little Ketchup-Head want her lunch-box back?" Jenny took another step forward. She was almost on Vicky's toes. She held up her polybag.

"I've got some lunch to put in my lunch-box," she said calmly. "Go and get it for me. Now."

Vicky was visibly stunned. She glanced at Sharon, who tried to move behind Jenny, but Jenny blocked her off. She no longer felt any fear; only a fiery power burning in her eyes, sparking like sword blade upon sword blade. Jenny glared at Sharon.

"Have you got a problem? Don't you know where it is?"

A grin spread across Sharon's face.

"Of course I know where it is. We all know where it is, don't we Vicky?" Now Vicky started to smirk as well, while Clare chewed her lip again.

"You'd better get it, then," suggested Jenny. Vicky gave a low bow.

"Come and fetch it, Your Excellency! It's no problem, is it Sharon?"

"No problem at all," sniggered her friend. Clare now looked as if she wished the ground would swallow her up. She could not bear to look her old friend in the eye.

All four set off across the playground and didn't stop until they reached the school pond. Vicky pointed triumphantly to the little grassy island in the centre.

"There it is. Help yourself, Ketchup-Head!"

Jenny peered at the island. She could just see part of the lunch-box in the long grass. She turned back to the giggling girls.

"Go on," crowed Sharon. "Help yourself!"

Jenny tried to stay calm.

"How did it get there?" she asked, coolly.

"Threw it there, didn't we?" Vicky said with a grin. Jenny looked back at the island and nodded.

"You'd better go and get it, then."

"You WHAT?"

"You'd better go and get it," repeated Jenny. "You put it there. You'll have to go and get it back." Jenny's eyes burned into Vicky. The tiger was ready to pounce.

"No way!" cried Vicky, backing off. Jenny's hand flashed out and grabbed Vicky's wrist.

"Go and get it now," she insisted. "Take off your shoes and socks."

Sharon sneered, "You can't make her. There are three of us and..."

"Two," blurted Clare, suddenly. Vicky and Sharon were flabbergasted. Clare's face was worried and her hands were trembling. But she went and stood beside her old friend. "There are two of us and two of you."

7
The secret of the bed

Jenny looked at Clare and grinned. She turned to the others.

"You'd better go and get my lunch-box, then," she said, for the third time. "Both of you."

Vicky stood for a moment, glaring at Jenny. Then she gave in. She sat down heavily, pulling Sharon

down with her.

"Come on," she hissed. "They mean it."

Jenny and Clare stood over them as they took off their shoes and socks. They slipped their pale feet into the cold pond water.

"Urgh! It's revolting! It's all squelchy and mucky…"

"I want my lunch-box," insisted Jenny. The two girls held on to each other and waded to the island, clutching their skirts above the water and squeaking with disgust. At last they reached the box and came back, stirring up great clouds of black, slimy mud.

They stood in the pond and handed up the lunch-box.

"Thank you," Jenny said, politely. She opened it up and put the polybag inside. "By the way, don't call me Ketchup-Head ever again. If you do, it will be the gangplank for you, and you know where you'll end up then."

Jenny tossed back her flaming hair, took Clare by the arm and walked off to the classroom. She knew that Sharon and Vicky would never bother her again. As for Clare, she had a lot to sort out with her old friend.

The day went well and Jenny went home from school feeling happier than she had done for weeks. Strangely enough, when she climbed into the pirate bed that night, nothing happened. There was no gentle creak, no wind on her face or slap of waves. Jenny lay back on her pillows and smiled. She whispered to the empty room, "Thank you, Snakehair."

Jenny gently ran her hand along the top of the headboard, stroking the ancient wood. There was a tiny "click". A small wooden panel sprang out, falling onto the pillow beside her. The secret cupboard! In an instant she was sitting up, staring into the little hidden hole in the wood. She put in one hand and her fingers touched something hard.

Jenny drew it out carefully. It was a small book with a tattered cover. She stared at the title. *Pirates of Yesteryear.*

Jenny leafed through the yellow pages. They fell open at a chapter headed "Famous pirates". Opposite this was a picture that almost made Jenny scream out loud. It showed a woman with flaming red hair coiling round her face. She stared out from the picture with burning black eyes.

Jenny raced through the words beneath the picture until her eye was caught by a single name – Snakehair. Hardly daring to breathe she read on.

"…one of the most successful pirates was Snakehair, so called because of the mass of red curls that writhed about her head. However, her real name was Jenny Lockhart and she lived…"